Lives

Saint Joseph
with Prayers and Devotions

Edited by
Mark Etling

**Regina
Press**

GW01091103

Nihil Obstat: Reverend Robert O. Morrissey, J.C.D.
                 Censor librorum
                 March 24, 2003

Imprimatur: Most Reverend William Murphy
                 Bishop of Rockville Centre
                 March 31, 2003

THE REGINA PRESS
10 Hub Drive
Melville, New York 11747

All rights reserved. No part of this publication may be reproduced or transmitted in any form or by any means, electronic or mechanical, including photocopying, recording, or any information storage and retrieval system, without permission in writing from the publishers.

© Copyright 2003 by The Regina Press.

Florentine Collection™, All rights reserved worldwide.
Imported exclusively by Malco.

Printed in U.S.A.

ISBN: 0-88271-158-X

Introduction

*B*ecause their lives were so extraordinary, it is tempting for us to think that the saints are somehow superhuman beings– endowed with far greater virtue, morality, and faith than the rest of us.

It is true that the saints lived outstanding lives in one way or another – whether in their compassion for the poor, their scholarship, their preaching ability, or their deep spirituality.

But the saints were not superhuman. In fact, quite the opposite is true. What makes the saints so extraordinary – and their lives so exemplary - is the very humanity they share with each of us. What they have done, we can do.

Saint Joseph, for example, is one of the most outstanding and beloved of all the saints. That is because he was such a profoundly *human* being – in his desire not to cause shame to Mary over the child she had conceived without him; in his wonderment about the meaning of the prophetic words of Simeon at the Presentation; in his anxiety while searching for the lost child Jesus in the Temple.

What makes men and women like St. Joseph

so special – what makes them saints - is the way they lived out their humanity. It was their virtue, their fidelity, their love for God and his people that set them on the path to sainthood.

As we reflect on the life of St. Joseph, and as we pray for his intercession, we should remember that Joseph is a saint – a holy man – not because he was superhuman, but because he was such a deeply human being.

The Life of St. Joseph

What little reliable information we have about St. Joseph is found in the Gospels of Matthew and Luke. Although the details of his life are scant and scattered, they reveal a man of strong character and great faith.

The Gospel of Matthew tells us that when Joseph learned of Mary's pregnancy, he decided to divorce her quietly. The two were already betrothed, which meant that the written contract of marriage had been drawn up. At that time, the Jewish marriage ceremony was not completed until the groom took the bride into his house. If Joseph had nullified the marriage contract at this point it would not have been considered divorce under Jewish law. Yet Matthew is careful to point out that Joseph wanted to spare Mary any public shame, and that he was "a just man" - he took his Jewish faith seriously and had a deep desire to observe the Law.

The story goes on to say that an angel appeared to Joseph in a dream and told him he need not divorce Mary, because the child she had conceived was of the Holy Spirit. Because he was a just man, Joseph obeyed the command of the angel when he awoke.

As the time for the birth of the child neared, the Gospel of Luke tells us that a census was declared by the Roman Emperor Caesar Augustus. Each family was to travel to its own native city to be enrolled. Joseph and Mary made the 90-mile trip from Nazareth to Bethlehem because it had been the native town of Joseph's royal ancestor, King David.

While they were in Bethlehem, the time came for Mary to bear her child. Because Joseph was a poor man, the child Jesus was probably born in one of the caves in the hills around Bethlehem and laid in a manger, a feeding trough for animals.

It is no wonder, then, that God revealed the birth of Jesus, the son of a poor man, first to poor shepherds working in the fields around Bethlehem. The Gospel of Luke declares that as the shepherds approached the cave, they found the Holy Family together, with Mary and Joseph lovingly caring for the child Savior.

Being devout Jews, it was natural for Joseph

and Mary to have Jesus circumcised and named eight days after his birth, and then to be purified as a family by observing the presentation ritual. The Gospel of Luke tells us that Joseph and Mary marveled when, during the presentation ceremony, Simeon took the baby in his arms and declared: "Lord, let your servant now depart in peace, according to your word; for my eyes have seen your salvation which you have prepared in the presence of all peoples, a light of revelation to the Gentiles, and of glory to your people Israel" (Luke 2:29-32).

Wise men from Persia would later come to pay homage and bring gifts to Jesus, after having observed his star at its rising. But they made the mistake of telling King Herod of their search for the "king of the Jews," and this enraged Herod. Once again, an angel appeared to Joseph in a dream and told him to take the child and his mother to Egypt, in order to escape Herod's wrath. The angry king ordered all the male children in Bethlehem killed. Only after the death of Herod did an angel tell Joseph to return to their native Israel, and to raise Jesus in Nazareth of Galilee.

As Joseph helped raise Jesus, he certainly must have passed on to the boy both the religious traditions of his Jewish faith and his technical skill as a carpenter. One of the religious customs observed by the Holy Family was the annual journey to Jerusalem at Passover. At the end of the celebration, the twelve-year-old Jesus stayed behind while Joseph and Mary started the return trip to Nazareth. When they discovered he was missing, they searched frantically for the boy for three days. Finally, they found him in the Temple, conversing with the learned men. When Mary asked why he had caused them such anxiety, Jesus replied only that he must be about his Father's business.

Even so, the Gospel of Luke points out that Jesus immediately returned home with Joseph and Mary and was obedient to them. This final reference to Joseph in the Gospels is a wonderful tribute to his quiet strength as a parent. Joseph never appears during Jesus' public ministry, which leads to the supposition that he had already died.

Even though there are few references to him in Sacred Scripture, and even though he is never quoted, Joseph surely must have been a strong and saintly man. The Gospels reveal a man of great faith, of heroic chastity, of courage in following the will of God, and of great love in seeking the happiness of his family before his own. This unassuming, seemingly ordinary carpenter from Nazareth was certainly a fitting foster father to the Son of God.

Prayers to St. Joseph

Prayer to St. Joseph

*B*lessed Joseph, husband of Mary,
   be with us today.
You protected and cherished the Virgin;
   loving the child Jesus as your Son,
   you rescued him from the danger of death.
Defend the Church, the family of God,
Redeemed by the blood of Christ.

Guardian of the Holy Family,
   be with us in our trials.
May your prayers obtain for us
   the strength to reject sin
   and reject the power of evil
   so that in life we may grow in holiness
   and in death rejoice in the crown of victory.
Amen.

Prayer to St. Joseph

*S*aint Joseph, whose protection is so great, so strong, and so prompt, I place in you all my interests and desires. St. Joseph, assist me by your powerful intercession and obtain for me, from your divine Son, spiritual blessings through Jesus Christ, our Lord.

Prayer to St. Joseph

(Ordered by Pope Leo XIII, to be prayed as part of the Devotions for the month of October.)

*T*o you, O blessed Joseph, we have recourse in our tribulations, and while imploring the aid of your most holy Spouse, we confidently invoke your patronage also. By that love which united you to the Immaculate Virgin Mother of God, and by the fatherly affection with which you did embrace the infant Jesus, we humbly ask you graciously to regard the inheritance which Jesus Christ purchased by his blood, and to help us in our necessities by your powerful intercession.

Protect, O most provident guardian of the

Holy Family, the chosen people of Jesus Christ; ward off from us, O most loving father, all taint of error and corruption; graciously assist us from heaven, O most powerful protector, in our struggle with the powers of darkness; and as you did once rescue the child Jesus from imminent peril to his life, so now defend the holy Church of God from the snares of her enemies and from all adversity. Shield each one of us with your unceasing patronage, that, imitating your example and supported by your aid, we may be enabled to live a good life, die a holy death, and secure everlasting happiness in heaven. Amen.

Prayer to St. Joseph

O blessed Saint Joseph, faithful guardian and protector of the Virgin, to whom God entrusted Jesus and Mary, I implore you by the love which you did bear them, to preserve me from every defilement of soul and body, that I may always serve them in holiness and purity of love. Amen.

Prayer To St. Joseph for Protection

*G*racious Saint Joseph, protect me and my family from all evil as you did the Holy Family. Kindly keep us ever united in the love of Christ, ever fervent in imitation of the virtue of our Blessed Lady, your sinless spouse, and always faithful in devotion to you. Amen.

Litany to St. Joseph

(Approved by Pope St. Pius X in 1909.)

*L*ord, have mercy on us.
Christ, have mercy on us.
Lord, have mercy on us.
Christ, hear us.
Christ, graciously hear us.

God, the Father of heaven, have mercy on us.
God, the Son, Redeemer of the world,
   have mercy on us.
God, the Holy Spirit, have mercy on us.
Holy Mary, pray for us.
St. Joseph, pray for us.
Blessed offspring of David, pray for us.

Light of patriarchs, pray for us.
Spouse of the mother of God, pray for us.
Chaste custodian of the Blessed Virgin,
   pray for us.
Guardian of the Son of God, pray for us.
Defender of Christ, pray for us.
Head of the Holy Family, pray for us.
O Joseph most just, pray for us.
O Joseph most chaste, pray for us.
O Joseph most prudent, pray for us.
O Joseph most forceful, pray for us.
O Joseph most obedient, pray for us.
O Joseph most faithful, pray for us.
Mirror of patience, pray for us.
Lover of poverty, pray for us.
Model of laborers, pray for us.
Patriarch of the home, pray for us.
Protector of virgins, pray for us.
Strength of the family, pray for us.
Comforter of the afflicted, pray for us.
Hope of the sick, pray for us.
Patron of the dying, pray for us.
Terror of demons, pray for us.
Protector of the Church, pray for us.

Lamb of God, you who take away the sins of the world, forgive us O Lord.

Lamb of God, you who take away the sins of the world, hear us O Lord.

Lamb of God, you who take away the sins of the world, have mercy on us.

Let us pray. Lord Jesus, through the merits of the devoted spouse of your most holy Mother, help us, we ask you, that what of ourselves we cannot obtain, may be granted through the intercession of the most holy patriarch, Saint Joseph. You who reign with God, the Father, in the unity of the Holy Spirit now and forever. Amen.

Prayer to St. Joseph

*B*lessed Joseph, loving husband of Mary, the immaculate Virgin Mother of God, and foster father of her Son, we turn to you with confidence as we pray for the Church throughout the world.

Watch over the family of God, redeemed by the precious blood of Christ, as you watched over the Holy Family of Nazareth.

You once rescued the child Jesus from the danger of death, protect now his people from the powers of darkness and strengthen it in every trial.

Give it your own courage in the struggle against evil, and keep it free from sin and error.

Help us to follow your example, that we may live a holy life, die a holy death, and so share your joy forever in heaven. Amen.

Prayer to St. Joseph

Holy Saint Joseph, foster father of Jesus and spouse of Mary, our immaculate Mother,

guardian of the Holy Family, I place you as head of our family here on earth.

Guard and protect us from all dangers in this life and place us in the arms of Jesus in the hour of our death. Amen

Thirty Days Prayer to Saint Joseph

Glorious St. Joseph, faithful guardian of Jesus Christ, to you we raise our hearts and hands to implore your powerful intercession in obtaining from Jesus all the help necessary for our spiritual and temporal welfare, particularly the blessing of a happy death and the special favor we now seek *(state request here)*.

Guardian of the Word Incarnate and chaste spouse of the Virgin Mary, we are alive with confidence that your prayers on our behalf will be graciously heard by God. Amen.

Prayer to St. Joseph

O Lord Jesus Christ who, by subjecting yourself to Mary and Joseph, consecrated family life with wonderful virtues, grant that by their help we may fashion our lives after the example of your Holy Family, and obtain everlasting fellowship with it. Who lives and reigns forever and ever. Amen.

Memorare to St. Joseph

*R*emember, O most chaste spouse of the Virgin Mary, that never was it known that anyone who implored your help and sought your intercession was left unassisted. Full of confidence in your power, I fly unto you, and beg your protection. Despise not, O foster father of the Redeemer, my humble supplication, but in your bounty, hear and answer me. Amen.

A Parent's Prayer to Saint Joseph

O glorious St. Joseph,
to you God committed the care
of His only begotten Son
amid the many dangers of this world.
We come to you and ask you to take under
our special protection
the children God has given us.
Through holy baptism
they became children of God
and members of his holy Church.
We consecrate them to you today,
that through this consecration
they may become your foster children.
Guard them, guide their steps in life,
form their hearts
after the hearts of Jesus and Mary.

St. Joseph,
who felt the tribulations and worry of a
parent when the child Jesus was lost,
protect our dear children for time and eternity.
May you be their father and counselor.
Let them, like Jesus,
grow in age as well as in wisdom and grace
before God and humanity.
Preserve them from the corruption
of this world,
and give us the grace one day to be united
with them in heaven forever. Amen

Prayer to St. Joseph

O glorious Saint Joseph,
through the love you bear to Jesus Christ,
and for the glory of his name,
hear our prayers,
and obtain our petitions.

Novena to St. Joseph

O glorious Saint Joseph,
faithful follower of Jesus Christ,
to you we raise our hearts and hands
to implore your powerful intercession
in obtaining from the gracious heart of Jesus
all the help and grace necessary
for our spiritual and temporal welfare,
particularly for the gift of a happy death
and the special favor we now request
(state request here).
O guardian of the Word Incarnate,
we feel animated with confidence that your
prayers on our behalf will be graciously
heard by God.

O glorious Saint Joseph,
through the love you bear to Jesus Christ
and for the glory of his name, hear our prayers
and obtain our petitions. Amen.

Day One

O great Saint Joseph,
with feelings of unlimited confidence,
we beg you to bless this novena that we

begin in your honor.
"You are never invoked in vain" says the
seraphic St. Theresa of Jesus.
Be then to me what you have been to that
spouse of the Sacred Heart of Jesus
and graciously hear me as you did her.
Amen.
St. Joseph, pray for us!

Day Two

O blessed Saint Joseph,
tenderhearted father,
faithful guardian of Jesus,
chaste spouse of the Mother of God,
we pray and ask you to offer to God the
Father, his divine Son, nailed to the
cross for sinners, and through the holy name
of Jesus obtain for us from the eternal Father
the favor for which we ask your intercession. . .
(state request here)
Amid the splendors of eternity,
forget not the sorrows of those who pray,
those who weep; stay your almighty arm,
that by your prayers and those of your most
holy spouse,

the Heart of Jesus may be moved to pity and
to pardon. Amen.
Saint Joseph, pray for us!

Day Three

*B*lessed Saint Joseph,
enkindle in our hearts the spark of your love.
May God always be the first
and only object of our love.
Keep our souls always in your grace and,
if we should be so unhappy as to lose it,
give us the strength to recover it
by our sincere repentance.
Help us to such a love for our God
That will keep us always united to him.
Amen.

O glorious Saint Joseph,
through your love for Jesus Christ
and for the glory of his name,
hear our prayers and obtain our petitions . . .
(state request here).

Day Four

Saint Joseph, pride of heaven,
unfailing hope for our lives,
and support of those on earth,
graciously accept our prayer of praise.
You were the chosen spouse of the chaste
Virgin by the Creator of the world.
He willed that you be called "father" of the
Word and serve as an agent of our salvation.
May the triune God who bestowed upon
you heavenly honors be praised forever.
And may he grant us through your merits
the joy of a blessed life and a favorable answer
to our petition . . . *(state request here).*
Amen.

Day Five

O holy Saint Joseph,
what a lesson your life is for us,
ever so eager to appear so anxious
to display before the eyes of humanity
the grace that we owe entirely to the
generous love of God.
In addition to the special favor for which we
pray in this novena . . . *(state request here)*

grant that we may attribute to God the glory
of all things, that we may love the humble and
hidden life, that we may not desire any other
position in life than the one given us by the
provident God and that we may always be
open to the will of God. Amen.
Saint Joseph, pray for us!

Day Six

O glorious Saint Joseph,
appointed by the eternal Father
as the guardian and protector of the life of
Jesus Christ, the comfort and support of his
holy Mother, and the instrument of his great
design for the redemption of the world;
you who had the happiness of living with
Jesus and Mary, and of dying in their arms,
be moved by the confidence we place in you,
and procure for us from the Almighty,
the particular favor which we humbly ask
through your intercession . . . *(state request here)*
Amen.
Saint Joseph, pray for us!

Day Seven

O faithful and prudent Saint Joseph,
watch over our weakness and
our inexperience; obtain for us that prudence
which reminds us of our end,
which directs our paths and which protects
us from every danger.
Pray for us, then, O great saint,
and by your love for Jesus and Mary,
and by their love for you,
obtain for us the favor we ask in this novena . . .
(state request here).
Amen.
Saint Joseph, pray for us!

Day Eight

O blessed Joseph,
to whom it was given not only to see
and to hear that God whom many kings
longed to see and saw not;
to hear and heard not;
but also to carry him in your arms,
to embrace him, to clothe him,
and to guard and defend him,
come to our assistance and intercede with him

to look favorably on our present situation . . .
(state request here).
Amen.
Saint Joseph, pray for us!

Day Nine

O good Saint Joseph, help us to be like you,
gentle to those whose weakness leans on us;
help us to give to those who seek our aid,
strength that they may journey unafraid.
Give us your faith, that we may see the right
shining above the victories of might.
Give us your hope that we may stand secure,
untouched by doubting, steadfast to endure.
Give us your love that as the years increase
an understanding heart may bring us peace.
Give us your purity that the hour of death
finds us untouched by evil's breath.
Give us your love of labor
that we shirk no lot in life that calls us for
honest work.
Give us your love of poverty so that we live
contented, letting wealth come or go.
Give us your courage that we may be strong;
give us your meekness to confess our sins.

Give us your patience that we may possess
the kingdom of our souls without distress.
Help us, dear saint,
to live so that when life ends
we pass with you to Jesus and his friends.

Glorious Saint Joseph,
hear our prayers and obtain our petitions.
Amen.
Saint Joseph, pray for us!

A Novena Prayer to Saint Joseph

O glorious descendant of the kings of Judah!
Inheritor of the virtues of all the patriarchs!
Just and happy Saint Joseph!
Listen to my prayer.
You are my glorious protector,
and shall ever be, after Jesus and Mary,
the object of my most profound veneration
and confidence.
You are the most hidden,
though one of the greatest saints,
and you are particularly the patron of those
who serve God with the greatest purity
and fervor.
In union with all those who have ever been
devoted to you,
I now dedicate myself to your service;
asking you, for the sake of Jesus Christ,
who consented to love and obey you as a son,
to become a father to me,
and to obtain for me the respect,
confidence, and love of a child towards you.
O powerful advocate of all Christians,
whose intercession, as St. Teresa assures us,

has never been found to fail,
intercede for me now,
and obtain for me the particular intention of
my novena . . . *(state intention here).*

Present me,
O great saint, to the blessed Trinity,
with whom you had so glorious and so
intimate a correspondence.
Grant that I may never deface by sin the
sacred image of your likeness,
in which I was created.
Intercede for me, that my divine Redeemer
would enkindle in my heart and in all hearts,
the fire of his love, and infuse in them the
virtues of his childhood,
his purity, simplicity, obedience, and humility.
Obtain for me likewise a devotion to your
Virgin spouse,
and protect me in life and death,
that I may have the happiness of dying as
you did, in the friendship of my Creator,
and under the protection of the
Mother of God.

Prayer to St. Joseph

Saint Joseph, father and guardian of virgins,
into whose faithful keeping Innocence itself
was entrusted, Christ Jesus,
and Mary, the Virgin of virgins,
I pray and ask you through Jesus and Mary,
those pledges so dear to you,
to keep me from all uncleanness,
and to grant that my mind may be untainted,
my heart pure and my body chaste;
help me always to serve Jesus and Mary in
perfect chastity.
Amen.

Prayer to St. Joseph

O blessed Saint Joseph,
faithful guardian and protector of virgins,
to whom God entrusted Jesus and Mary,
I ask you by the love which you bore them
to preserve me from every defilement of soul
and body, that I may always serve them in
holiness and purity of love.
Amen.

Prayer to St. Joseph

O blessed Joseph,
faithful guardian of my Redeemer, Jesus
Christ, protector of your chaste spouse,
the virgin Mother of God, I choose you this
day to be my special patron and advocate
and I firmly resolve to honor you all
the days of my life.
Therefore I humbly ask you to receive me as
your friend, to instruct me in every doubt,
to comfort me in every affliction,
to obtain for me and for all the knowledge
and love of the Heart of Jesus,
and finally to defend and protect me at the
hour of my death. Amen.

Prayer to St. Joseph

O Saint Joseph, whose protection is so great,
so strong, so prompt before the throne of God,
I place in you all my interest and desires.
O Saint Joseph, do assist me by your
powerful intercession, and obtain for me
from your divine Son all spiritual blessings

through Jesus Christ, our Lord.
So that, having engaged here below your
heavenly power,
I may offer my thanksgiving and homage to
the most loving of Fathers.
O Saint Joseph, I never weary contemplating
you, and Jesus asleep in your arms; I dare not
approach while he reposes near your heart.
Press him in my name and kiss his fine head
for me and ask him to return the kiss
when I draw my dying breath.
St. Joseph, patron of departed souls,
pray for me.
*(In 1505, this prayer was sent from Pope Julius II
to Emperor Charles, when he was going into battle.)*